SEAS

SAVING SPACE ONE PLANET AT A TIME

Star Girl is first published in the United States in 2015
by Picture Window Books
A Capstone imprint
1710 Roe Crest Drive
North Mankato, Minnesota 56003
www.capstonepub.com

Library of Congress Cataloging-in-Publication Data is available on the Library of
Congress website.

ISBN: 978-1-4795-8277-8 (library binding)
ISBN: 978-1-4795-8281-5 (paperback)
ISBN: 978-1-4795-8473-4 (eBook PDF)

Summary: An underwater world is being poisoned and the aquamantas are getting
sick. Star Girl is eager to help, but she soon discovers that looks can be deceiving. Can
the space cadets find the source of the poison and stop it in time to save the planet and
its inhabitants?

Designer: Natascha Lenz

This *Winning Moves* US Edition is published by arrangement with Macmillan
Education Australia Pty Ltd, 15 - 19 Claremont Street, South Yarra, Vic 3141,
Australia

Printed in the United States of America by Corporate Graphics

STAR GIRL
SAVING SPACE ONE PLANET AT A TIME

WINNING MOVES

LOUISE PARK

PICTURE WINDOW BOOKS
a capstone imprint

SPACE EDUCATION

Protective Dome

Horse Riding Club

Boys' Dorm

Dome Traveler

Space Tube

Repair Center

Classrooms

Stabilizer Units

FlyBy

Spaceball Court

Docking Bays

The Comet Café

Celebration Holopods

Movie Theater and Bowling Hub

Energy Core

AND ACTION SCHOOL

Staff Only Zone

Staff Quarters

Space Tube

Girls' Dorm

Gymnasium and Ballet Studio

Classrooms

Agricultural Center

Space Flight Training Center

Docking Bays

Escape Pod

Beach Island

SEAS

A SPACE STATION BOARDING SCHOOL FOR GIRLS AND BOYS

The Space Education and Action School is located on Space Station Edumax. Students in the space training program complete space missions on planets in outer space that are in danger and need help.

Not all students will make it through to their final year and only the best students will go on to become space agents. Addie must make it through and become a Space Agent. Outer space needs her.

Program: Space Cadetship

Student: Adelaide Banks

Space Cadet: Star Girl

Age: 10 years old

School house: Stellar

Space missions: 2

Earned mission points: 14

Earned house points: 91

Comments: Adelaide completed her second cadet mission and did very well. She has also recently joined the school spaceball team and is demonstrating a better team attitude. However, she continues to struggle with some of her subjects and needs to get better grades in order to keep her cadetship.

Note to all staff: Adelaide prefers to be called Addie.

CHAPTER ONE

Addie was at the spaceball courts and feeling very nervous. Ms. Styles, the ballet teacher, had talked her into trying out for the spaceball team, and the next thing Addie knew, she was goalie for Stellar house. Addie was wearing her new spaceball grip gloves, grip boots, and uniform.

"Goalie!" Addie moaned. "Why did I have to be goalie?"

"Stop stressing out," Olivia said. "You're starting to make me feel nervous. I'm already a little scared about playing Nebula. Anyway, goalie is a good position."

Miya gave Addie a hug. "Addie, you were picked because you do great leaps pushing off from the floor in ballet. Once the game starts just pretend you're in ballet class, except when you push off from the floor, it's to get a ball and stop it from hitting the scoreboard."

"I just don't feel like I've had enough time on the court," said Addie.

"All you have to do is stop the ball from hitting the scoreboard," Olivia said.

"Just keep your eye on the ball the whole time," added Miya. "The Nebula players will pass the ball to each other and try to get close to your goal area. You have to be alert and ready to block their ball. That's it!"

"I know," said Addie. "It's just that I'm still getting used to the whole no gravity thing in there. I like the way the space station has its own gravity."

"You've had tons of experience with no gravity in Zero Gravity classes," Miya said.

"Yeah, but I got a big fat D on my last Zero Gravity test." Addie groaned. "I didn't even know that you have to attach yourself to a toilet to use it or you'll just float away! I'm doing pretty bad in Space 101 and Elemental Galaxy too. I'm just kind of stressed out right now with everything, I think. I'd better get in there and warm up. See you, Miya."

Miya smiled. "I'll be cheering you on."

Addie stood in the goal area. She pushed off from the bottom of the court and began soaring upward. *It feels like swimming,* she thought. *Just like when I push off from the wall under the water in the pool at home.* She traveled upward until she touched the spaceball court roof above her with her hands. She floated.

Olivia was shooting practice balls at Addie. She used her grip shoes to walk up the wall of the court. She pushed her big toes down on the buttons inside her shoes that released the grip. Holding the ball, she pushed off and headed for the opposite side.

Addie watched her closely.

On her way past the goal area, Olivia threw the ball straight at the scoreboard.

Addie pushed off from the roof with her hands and headed for where she thought the ball was headed. But she pushed off too hard and shot down to the floor. Reaching for the ball, she missed it completely.

Addie touched down on the floor with her grip boots. She was about to push off when she heard a loud voice. Addie glanced up. It was Sabrina, a player for Nebula.

"This will be an easy win for Nebula. Stellar's goalie is hopeless!" Sabrina told Valentina.

"Yeah," said Valentina. "We'll make every goal we try for, and *they* won't score any with me as Nebula goalie. And it's a hundred school house points for the winning team. Nebula needs those right now."

Mr. Rook blew his whistle. "The game will start in one minute, girls," he said.

Sabrina and Olivia went to the center circle and waited.

Mr. Rook blew the whistle and threw the ball up in the air. Both girls pushed off from the floor in a race to get to it first. Olivia grabbed it and threw it forward. Two more girls pushed off from the sides. One was from Stellar and the other from Nebula. Nebula grabbed the ball, and before Addie knew it, the ball was heading down toward the goal she was defending. Sabrina pushed off from high up on the wall at an angle. She was headed right for the scoreboard.

Addie moved fast. She guessed the flight path of the ball as it left Sabrina's hands and pushed off from the floor.

Please let me get this, she thought as she flew up toward the roof. Suddenly her gloves made contact with the ball. She grabbed it and threw it down the court. *Phew!*

But the ball was caught again by Nebula.

"Get ready," Aneliese yelled to Grace, her Nebula teammate, as she shot the ball down the court toward the Stellar goal area again. Grace pushed down from the roof and somersaulted toward the ball. She caught it and threw it so fast that Addie didn't have a chance. The ball hit the scoreboard and the bell rang out.

Then the new score appeared on both scoreboards.

NEBULA   STELLAR

1   0

"Sorry, Ads," mouthed Grace.

Addie smiled. "Good goal," she called back. Then she looked down the court at Valentina. She was at the other end in her goal area, laughing. *Laughing at me, I guess,* thought Addie.

Then the scoreboards flashed again.

MIYAKO WAKUDA, ADELAIDE BANKS, VALENTINA ADAMS, AND SABRINA SIMCIC

REPORT TO THE FLYBY

"Samantha Winter, you're on," called Mr. Rook. "Off you go, Addie, and don't look so happy to be out of the game."

"Well, I wasn't exactly great out there, was I?" Addie mumbled.

"You blocked one goal and another got through," said Mr. Rook. "I'd say you did a pretty good job. I'm looking forward to seeing more goalie work from you. Good luck with your mission."

"Thanks, Mr. Rook," said Addie, feeling a little better about her efforts. "Good luck, Sam. I hope we win."

CHAPTER TWO

Addie and Miya hurried to the FlyBy.

"I think I need to practice that game more," said Addie.

"Nebula needs to win that game," said Miya. "Have you seen the school's house points lately? Nova is in the lead now and Nebula is second. Valentina's angry about it. She loves being the best. Her house isn't in first place anymore, and she's not the number one space cadet anymore either. Grace is. I wonder where Valentina and Sabrina are, anyway?

They were called to the FlyBy too."

"I don't know," Addie said. "You don't think we'll have to go on a mission with them, do you?"

"No. We always go in pairs," said Miya. "I hope we get to go together."

"I bet I get Valentina as my partner again," said Addie as they arrived at the FlyBy's door. "Maybe she and Sabrina are already inside. We'd better get in there too. You do your Face Scan first."

"Let's see if we can do it together," Miya said with a grin. "It'll be like having our photos taken in those photo booths at home. We can make funny faces. Ready?"

"Ready," said Addie. The girls huddled

close together in front of the FlyBy door's security screen. Addie opened her mouth really wide and made her eyes bulge, and Miya made an even sillier face.

The door beeped and swung open. Addie and Miya were laughing so hard that they almost fell through the doorway.

"I love that photo," said Addie.

"Good morning, space cadets," said Professor Nebulas, turning toward them. "So glad you could join us."

Addie and Miya stopped laughing and straightened themselves up.

He looks soooo old, thought Addie. *No wonder he is the only teacher here that has a school house named after him.* Then Addie remembered that Professor Nebulas was one of the four teachers who founded SEAS and began its space agent program. *I wonder where the other three founding teachers are now?*

"Hello, Professor," Miya said.

Addie saw Valentina and Sabrina were already there. They looked at Miya and Addie as though they were silly little kids.

"As I was saying," said Professor Nebulas, turning back to Valentina and Sabrina, "I was not happy to be calling two of our best Nebula spaceball players to the FlyBy during a game. But missions come first. All right, Ms. Styles is waiting in Briefing Room 2 to brief you, so off you go. Do your best and make your house proud."

Sabrina and Valentina left the room and Professor Nebulas turned back to Miya and Addie. "No offense, girls, but I do have to support my own house."

"Of course, Professor," said Miya.

"You'll be going on a different mission," he continued. "We're headed for the space tank simulators."

"Space tank simulators? What are they?" asked Addie.

"They're these weird tanks where it's just like you're underwater, but you're not," said Miya. "We must be going to a planet with lots of water."

"Correct, Astron," said the professor. "You'll be going to the galaxy of Novanellan and a small water-covered planet called Aquare. Something is polluting the yellow water there. Come this way, please."

The girls followed the professor into a room that had three chambers that were connected to a central computer. Each one had a glass door that opened upward. "Are these the tanks? They look like pods," said Addie.

"Yes, but once you are inside we can create a whole underwater experience with the computers. It will help prepare you for the mission. There are your underwater spacesuits," said the professor, pointing to two suits hanging up against the wall of the changing rooms.

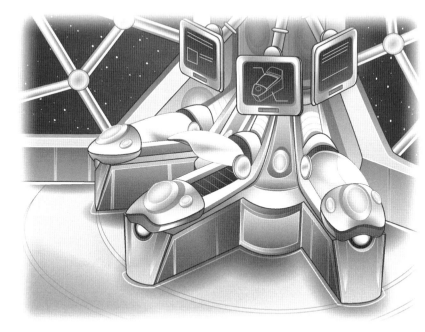

Addie and Miya helped each other put their suits on in the changing rooms.

"They're just like normal spacesuits," Addie said, "except they're hot pink!"

"Yeah, we definitely won't lose each other!" Miya laughed. "The bottom of the legs are kind of weird. They have feet. And the sleeves have built-in gloves."

"The only thing they don't cover is our heads," said Addie.

"You'll need these special helmets for that," said Professor Nebulas, overhearing the girls as they walked back into the room. He was holding two see-through helmets. "The underwater environment of Aquare is toxic to humans."

"Our normal helmets and suits aren't enough for us to survive in those waters. You'll both have flip-jets and aqualungs as well. The water is thicker than ours. You will find it very hard to move through. The flip-jets will propel you through the water and the aqualungs will allow you to breathe."

AQUALUNGS AND FLIP-JETS

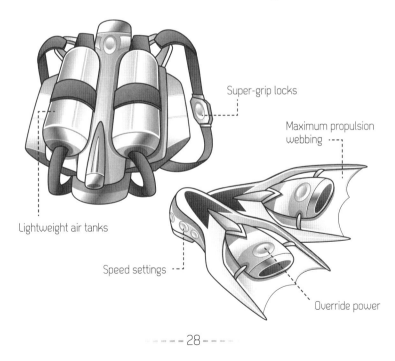

Super-grip locks

Maximum propulsion webbing

Lightweight air tanks

Speed settings

Override power

"How do we work the jets on the flippers?" asked Miya.

"I'll load the jet controls into the touch screen computer on your holographic watches. I'll check your GPS tracking chips and load myself into the holograph at the same time. May I have your watches, please? I'll set them while you girls are in the tanks."

SCHOOL ISSUE HOLOGRAPHIC WATCH

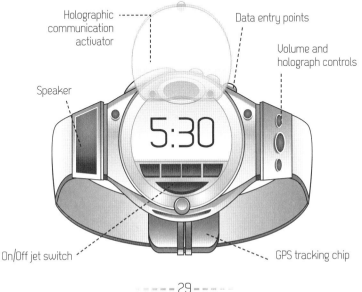

Holographic communication activator

Data entry points

Volume and holograph controls

Speaker

On/Off jet switch

GPS tracking chip

Every cadet at SEAS had a holographic watch with a GPS tracking chip. When students were on a mission, teachers could locate them at all times using the tracking chip. Students could also call up their holographic teacher for help using the holographic contact under the watch's cover.

"Once I turn on the simulator, the tank will look and feel just like the environment of Aquare," the professor explained. "You won't need to research this planet. You will have the complete experience in the tanks. In you go, girls."

Addie and Miya each climbed into a tank.

"We'll be able to talk to each other the whole time," said the professor. "Okay, we're all set. I'm closing the lids now."

Addie lay very still as her tank lid came down over her pod and closed.

"I'm starting the simulator now, girls," Professor Nebulas said into the tank's microphone.

Suddenly, Addie felt as if she was floating. *Weird, it's like being in the spaceball courts,* she thought. She went to move her arms.

"It feels like I'm pushing against a big force," she said.

"Yes," said the professor. "Moving through Aquare's waters will make you very tired without help from the flip-jets that we've given you. I'm turning on the Aquare environment."

Inside Addie's tank, everything went a strange yellow color. Then she saw blue sand and rocks. Suddenly out from behind a rock swam a large creature. It came straight at Addie and she screamed.

"That's an aquamanta but it isn't real, Star Girl," the professor said. "It's a simulation, remember."

"It's so ugly!" Addie said. "It's like a cross between a Jell-O, a caterpillar, and a super-gross fish." The creature had multiple legs, sunken eyes, and a huge mouth.

Then before Addie knew it, her tank seemed to be filled with the creatures in all shapes and sizes. She slowly lifted her hand to touch one of them, but there was nothing there. *That's right,* she thought. *This is a simulation, even though it looks and feels so real!*

"I'm switching the simulator off," said the professor. "You must get going. Those beautiful alien life forms you've just seen are being destroyed by a sticky purple goo. We need you to find out where it is coming from."

Beautiful life forms? Addie thought, surprised by the professor's choice of words. Then everything that she could see inside the tank suddenly disappeared and she looked out through the glass into the room again.

The doors of the tanks opened and the girls climbed out.

"Here are your helmets," said Professor Nebulas.

"You'll be traveling with SA Space Surfer in the *Saturn 6*. Your mission packs and other equipment are waiting for you on board, and Space Surfer will finish briefing you."

Addie and Miya followed the professor to a docking bay where *Saturn 6* was parked. The spacecraft's doors were already open.

"Good luck, girls, and don't forget to work as a team," said the professor. "Call me on the holograph if you need to ask anything."

CHAPTER THREE

Saturn 6 wasn't like any rocket or shuttle that Addie had ever seen. It was a sphere and it had rings around it. "I can see where it got its name," said Addie. "It looks like the planet Saturn with those rings around it."

"I've been in it once before," said Miya. "The rings and its round shape allow it to float on the surface of water planets. It's a pretty cool spacecraft."

The girls stepped inside and locked their helmets and aqualungs into the holding bays.

SATURN 6

"I love these chairs or beds or whatever they are!" said Addie, and she collapsed into one of them. "They are so comfy, plus we have our own screens."

"Glad you like it, Star Girl," said Space Surfer over the cabin intercom from the cockpit. "Good morning and welcome to you and Astron. Buckle up, please. Takeoff is in two minutes. We're in a little bit of a rush today."

"How long is the flight to Aquare?" asked Miya.

"It will be about twenty minutes," said Space Surfer. "Your in-flight screens will be taking you through the equipment in your mission packs. Ready for takeoff?"

"Ready," said Miya after she checked that everything was stored away correctly.

The *Saturn 6* shot out from the space station's docking bay. Addie looked out her window and watched as in seconds the space station boarding school shrank away until she couldn't see it anymore. "Wow, we're really moving fast!"

"Yep, this thing can go," answered Miya.

"The in-flight briefing is about to start, space cadets," said Space Surfer again through the cabin speakers.

The girls opened their mission packs and took out what was inside.

"It looks like they packed these for a sleepover or something. What is all this stuff?" asked Miya.

Addie looked inside her mission pack. "I have something kind of like a hair dryer and a can of hair spray," she said. She looked across at Miya's equipment. "And it looks like you have hair styling gel and hair clips. Maybe we're supposed to do our hair on the way to Aquare."

The girls laughed as their screens flashed

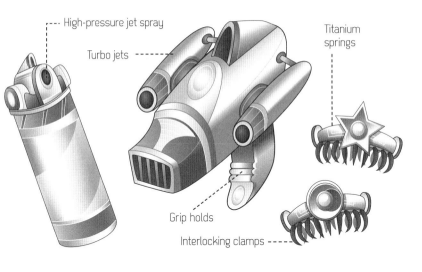

High-pressure jet spray

Turbo jets

Titanium springs

Grip holds

Interlocking clamps

REPELLENT, BLOWER, AND CLIPS

on and the briefing began. They settled down and watched their screens quietly. When it was finished Addie said, "So, the dryer thing has really strong blowing power. I don't know what we'd use that for."

"Yeah, or what the Aquare water-resistant heavy duty clips are for," said Miya. "But the spray will come in handy for sure. It repels things. Hopefully it will repel those scary aquamantas! Or maybe it can repel the goo that the professor said is polluting the water."

"That goo sounds really bad," said Addie. "I hope it doesn't damage our suits. The briefing video said there were spare suits in the launching bay. I wonder what color they are."

"Probably pink, too," said Miya.

Space Surfer's voice came through the cabin speakers. "Five minutes until we reach the Novanellan galaxy, space cadets. You might want to come up to the cockpit to see this. I think it's the most awesome galaxy in space."

The girls undid their seat belts and walked up to the cabin door. The door sprang open and the girls stood staring, their mouths wide open like the alien fish on Aquare.

The cockpit window wrapped around the front of *Saturn 6*. The view was incredible!

"The Novanellan galaxy is a rainbow of colors and shaped like a seahorse lying on its side," said Space Surfer. "Planet Aquare is in its tail."

"It's magical," said Miya. She took out her

SpaceBerry and took a photo of it.

"Good idea," said Addie, who was still getting used to having her own school-issued cell phone with a camera in it. "I'll send this photo home to my friend, Jess."

"Show's over now, cadets," said Space Surfer. "We're going in and will touch down on Aquare very soon."

"Thanks, Space Surfer," the girls said, and they headed back to their seats for landing.

Addie looked out her window again. A planet was coming into view, and it looked like it was on fire. "Aquare," she said. "It's weird that it's so yellow. I know it's outer space, but I just expect a water planet to be blue."

Outside, *Saturn 6*'s rings seemed to fill with air like an inflatable. Then it gently set down on a bright yellow sea and floated like a boat.

"Okay, cadets," said Space Surfer as he stepped into the cabin, "grab your helmets, aqualungs, and mission packs, and follow me down to the launching bay."

The girls followed Space Surfer down some stairs to another area with a long wall at the back of it. He keyed in a code on the wall's security pad.

A door slid open and they stepped inside the launching bay. Space Surfer helped the girls with their helmets and strapped on their aqualungs. "Check to make sure the controls for the flip-jets on your watches are working."

"Done," the girls replied as they attached their flip-jets to their suited feet.

"Then you're good to go," said Space Surfer. "There's a button on the outside to open the doors when you want to come back inside. Good luck, space cadets. I'll wait here until you return." He stepped back inside the lower cabin and closed the door behind him.

"Let's do it," said Miya. She hit the release button on the outer wall. The doors opened and they dived into a brilliant yellow sea.

CHAPTER ★ FOUR

The sea was thick and it was hard to move in. The girls floated in it and looked around. "Look at those weird blue rocks and that sand," said Addie. "And all those strange yellow weeds and stuff."

"There are also lots of caves and underwater caverns, right?" said Miya. "We need to activate our flip-jets so we can get moving." But Addie didn't reply. She was too busy looking around. "Addie," Miya yelled. "Turn your flip-jets on so we can get going."

"But look at all these alien creatures lying on the seafloor," said Addie floating in the sea. "They're covered in that purple stuff, and they aren't moving."

"I know," said Miya. "But we can't help them until we find out what this purple stuff is and where it's coming from."

Addie fired up her jets and the girls cruised through the water. There were huge blobs of purple stuff on the blue sand, rocks, and underwater cliffs. There weren't any aquamantas swimming in the water like there had been in the tank. The sea was empty.

"This is weird," Addie said.

"The aliens on the seafloor that are covered with purple goo can't be all of them.

There has to be more somewhere else," said Miya.

As the girls cruised along, the amount of purple goo increased. It was floating in the water all around them.

Addie and Miya dodged and ducked the blobs of purple that were flying at them, but they were coming thicker and faster. Suddenly a blob hit Addie in the leg. It stuck to her like glue. She looked up at Miya. She'd been hit on her back. Then Addie noticed strange purple smoke coming off where she'd been hit.

The same smoke was coming from Addie's leg.

"Miya, the purple stuff is melting our suits!" Addie yelled.

"Quick, we have to get back to the launching bay."

The girls turned their flip-jets to full blast and powered through the water to *Saturn 6*. Miya hit the button to open the launching bay doors and the girls fell inside.

"This stuff is bad," said Addie as she pulled her suit off and threw her mission pack out of the way. "Look, it's melting the whole suit to nothing!"

The girls watched as their suits melted away to a purple puddle on the floor.

"It's just the suit material, though," said Miya. "It's not doing anything to the launching bay floor. Lucky we have spare suits, but how are we going to avoid all that purple stuff? Do you think that spray would work?"

"I'm not sure," Addie answered.

"Hey," said Miya. "I got a school ribbon in my hair. We could try it on that." Miya took the ribbon and sprayed it. Then she threw it on the purple puddle on the floor. Nothing happened. "Will we do it?" she asked.

"Yep," said Addie thinking of those aliens lying on the seafloor. "I'll get the spare suits."

She opened the storage bay. "If you thought we wouldn't lose each other in the pink suits, wait till you see these!" she said, pulling one out and handing it to Miya. They both burst out laughing. "Pink with purple hearts and yellow daisies!" said Addie. "But they are kind of cute."

"As long as they work," said Miya. "Let's get them sprayed and put them on."

When the girls were dressed, they stood in the launching bay ready to go out again.

"I'm still scared it won't work," said Addie.

"Me too," said Miya, shaking a little as she hit the button to open the doors.

The girls dived into the water and toward the oncoming purple goo.

"It's working," said Addie. "Our suits seem to be safe."

"But for how long?" Miya called back.

As they swam, more and more goo filled the water, and they saw more and more aliens on the seafloor covered in it.

"It's getting so hard to move forward," said Addie.

"But we have to keep going," said Miya.

"Yes," agreed Addie as she struggled on. "If the purple stuff is getting thicker, this has to be the way."

Suddenly the water ahead went very dark.

"What's that?" asked Miya.

"It looks like a massive island of goo!" yelled Addie. "And it's coming straight for us."

The girls looked around frantically. Then Miya pointed at a huge cavern in the blue rocks to their left. "Quick! Let's go."

But as they swam toward the cave, they saw hundreds of scary sunken eyes staring out at them from the darkness of the cave.

"Um . . . it looks a little too crowded in there," said Addie.

Miya looked from the cave to the purple goo headed their way. "We don't have any choice," she urged. "That stuff will cover us and we'll end up on the seafloor."

But Addie just kept staring at the cave.

"Hurry, or we won't make it," Miya yelled. She grabbed Addie's arm and pulled her into the cave with only seconds to spare.

From the cave's entrance, they floated in the water and watched as the massive blob of purple goo floated past. The sea turned an eerie dark color. Addie was glad she wasn't out there—until she looked behind her and saw what she was sharing a cave with.

CHAPTER FIVE

The huge cavern was jam-packed with Aquare
life forms of all sizes. Their mouths were open
and their legs were dangling in the yellow
water.

"If I wasn't so scared I might think they
were beautiful," Addie said with a tremble.

Up close and real the Aquare aliens were
spectacular in a weird alien sort of way.

Their eyes were a shiny golden yellow,

 and they had scales

covering their large

Jell-O-like shapes that shimmered with bright colors. There was an extremely large and old-looking one floating nearby.

"Let me try the translator app on my SpaceBerry," said Addie. "I used it with Grace and we could understand what the aliens were saying." Addie clicked on the app.

"We won't hurt you," the deep gurgling voice said through the SpaceBerry speaker. "We know who you are."

Addie let out a long anxious breath and smiled. "That's good to know," she said. "Because it looks like we are all stuck in here together."

"We cannot leave," said the ancient alien. "It is not safe for us out there. But we are running out of food and cannot stay here much longer either."

"The purple stuff just keeps coming," said Miya. "We are going to have to find where it's coming from and stop it." Just then the current pushed a big blob of purple toward the cave entrance.

Desperately, Addie leaned back and aimed her flip-jets at the purple goo. She blasted it with her jets at full-throttle. The goo was pushed back out into the sea, and Addie was thrown back among the alien creatures. Hundreds of tiny legs grabbed her and held her, stopping her from crashing into the cavern wall.

"Good thinking, Ads," said Miya. "And that gives me another idea. We can use that hair dryer gadget with the strong blowing power to repel the goo!"

"Yes, the blower," agreed Addie as all the little alien legs let go of her. "Thanks, guys," she said as she took the blower out of her mission pack. "Let's try it."

The girls moved out of the cave. Addie used the blower to clear the purple blobs.

Several of the older aquamantas followed behind with their hundreds of tiny legs propelling them rapidly through the thick sea.

"Now I know why they have so many legs," Addie laughed.

"Yeah," said Miya. "They don't need jets like we do."

The group moved through the sea in the direction of the purple goo. Addie pushed the purple goo aside with the blower as they went.

"The purple stuff is coming thick and fast now," said Addie, struggling to blow it out of the way.

"But look up ahead," said Miya.

There was a strange shape sticking up from the seafloor.

"That must be the source," said Addie.

"We can help," said the ancient aquamanta. "We can hold you and you can lean back and use your jets. Then you will have more power to blow the goo back."

"But it isn't safe for you here," Addie said. "You should go back to the cave."

"It won't be safe for us anywhere soon," the creature said. "Helping you will help us."

"Okay, let's do it," said Miya. "Lean back, Ads, and let's blast this stuff."

The two biggest creatures held Addie and Miya. Others pushed the large ones forward like supersized armchairs.

The girls' jets and the blower combined to make an enormous blast. All the purple goo was pushed away and they could see where it was coming from.

"It looks a little like the deep sea oil rigs at home," said Addie. "It's pumping the purple stuff from deep down in the seafloor. And it's sprung a leak!"

"And it has crab-like bots all over it," said Miya. "What are they doing?"

"Who knows," said Addie. "But we need to stop that leak before more aquamantas get coated with this stuff."

The girls looked at their new friends gathered behind them. Their little legs were waving in the sea and their mouths were open, but they weren't scary anymore.

"You're right," agreed Miya. "We have those water-resistant clips. They might clamp that tear. You can blow the stuff out of the way and I could try and clamp the leak."

"And what do we do about those nasty-looking crab-things with the huge pincers?" asked Addie.

"Good question," answered Miya.

"We can take care of them," said the ancient creature, "but only for a short time. You will have to work fast."

Addie continued to blow the purple goo away from the group, and the creatures moved out from behind her into the clean water. They lined up in a long row in front of the girls. Hundreds and hundreds of tiny legs went at top speed as they dug a deep trench in the bright blue sand.

The crab-bots stopped what they were doing and looked over. They crawled down from the structure and marched toward the creatures.

When the crab-bots reached the trench,

they fell in and the aquamantas began digging like crazy again. This time they put the blue sand back into the trench and filled it up.

"They will crawl their way out quickly," said the ancient creature. "You must hurry."

The girls moved as fast as they could. Addie pointed the blower at the gaping hole in the pump. It blew the purple goo away from them.

Miya took out the clips and went close to the pump. "It's some kind of rubber," she said, quickly clamping the hole. "It's working, but I don't know if it will hold it together for long."

"I hope it does," said Addie, "because the crabs are almost out of the trench, and they'll be coming right for us."

"Hey, what about this gel stuff that I have?" said Miya. "Maybe it's like glue."

"Squirt it on and see," said Addie.

Miya covered the clamped area with some of the gel, and then she and Addie swam back to the aquamantas, who carried the girls away.

Addie and Miya watched as the crab-bots crawled up out of the hole and back onto the structure.

"I think they are there to keep creatures away from it and that's all," said Addie.

"I think you're right," said Miya as she took her SpaceBerry out of her mission pack. "I'm just going to get a photo of this."

"I'll call Professor Nebulas on my holographic watch," said Addie. "I want to see if there's anything we can do for the sick aquamantas on the seafloor."

"Go for it," said Miya.

Addie looked up. She was a bit shocked. It was the first time her mission partner agreed to call the mission teacher. "Are you sure? You don't mind, Miya?"

"Totally not! Why would I?" she answered.

"I'll tell you later," Addie said as she opened her watch cover. Immediately, her teacher was there in holographic form.

"Star Girl, what's wrong and how can I help?" asked the professor.

"We found where the purple stuff was coming from and we stopped it. But we don't know for how long."

"Yes, I've been listening in with that new device in your watches. Good work on stopping the leak," said the professor. "But don't worry. Those aren't ordinary clips you've used, Star Girl. They are our heavy-duty water-resistant clamps. They will hold the

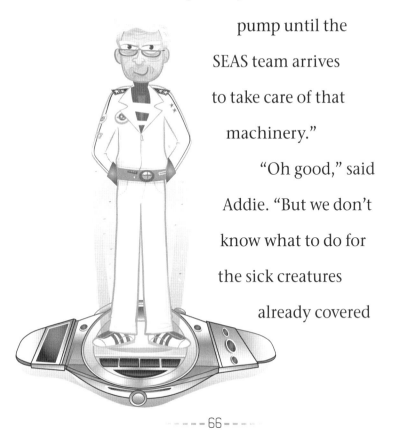

pump until the SEAS team arrives to take care of that machinery."

"Oh good," said Addie. "But we don't know what to do for the sick creatures already covered in the goo. Is there anything we can do to help them?"

"The gel should help heal them," said the professor. "I don't think it will do much good on the torn pump but good try! By the way, great mission, cadets. I've just let Space Surfer know you are ready to be picked up, and he will be above you any minute. We'll send a team in to follow up on your good work." Then Professor Nebulas was gone.

"Did you hear that, Miya?" Addie asked.

"I did." Miya laughed. "I'm glad I didn't waste too much of the gel on that pump!"

"Let's try it," said Addie. "I'll use the translator app to explain the gel to the ancient aquamantas."

The girls explained what they were going to do, then began squirting gel on the aquamantas on the seafloor. They moved quickly from one to the next.

"Look, Miya," Addie said, laughing. "All those little legs are handy for lots of things!"

Miya smiled as she watched her new friends use their hundreds of legs to rub gel into the bodies of the sick creatures. "They are really helpful," she said, "but I'm not sure how much more gel I have left."

Just then a round dark shape cast a shadow over the girls.

Addie looked up. "Space Surfer is here to take us home," she said.

"We'll have to give the gel to our ancient

friend here," said Miya. "It's time to go, and he knows what to do."

The girls handed the gel to the huge aquamanta and then they hit the icon on their watches to start up their flip-jets.

The old aquamanta closed its mouth over Addie's wrist. "It turned my flip-jets off," Addie said. "It must not want us to leave."

Suddenly Addie was on her back resting on hundreds of tiny little feet. "Hey, Miya," she called. "I think they're going to give me a ride!"

"Me too," said Miya as the creature flipped her onto her back. Laughing, the girls floated on their backs and were bumped along as the creatures carried them through the thick yellow sea to *Saturn 6.*

Space Surfer was waiting in the launching bay for the cadets when they arrived. He was dressed in a pink suit with yellow daisies and purple love hearts just like they were.

"Good job, cadets," he said with a grin. "And no comments about my suit. It's the only way I could greet you safely in case I got splashed."

Addie and Miya floated in front of Space Surfer and laughed.

"What a great photo opportunity," said Addie, taking out her SpaceBerry.

Space Surfer quickly grabbed Addie's SpaceBerry from her. "Of you two and your new alien friends," he said. "Big smiles, please. From all of you."

Addie and Miya floated together with the aquamantas until the camera clicked.

CHAPTER SIX

Back at the FlyBy, the girls were laughing with Professor Nebulas about their suits.

"Yes, one of our scientists creates very useful fabrics," he explained. "But she also loves bright colors and patterns! As long as they work, that's all that matters."

"We'll miss those creatures," said Miya. "We had a lot of fun with them while we were waiting for Space Surfer."

"They were very happy with the way you girls helped them," the professor said.

"SEAS is also very happy with you. You showed good judgment, smart thinking, and you worked well together. You will certainly earn high points."

At the mention of points, Addie suddenly remembered the spaceball game. "Who won the spaceball match, Professor?" she asked.

"Nebula, 3–1," the professor said with a grin. "Valentina and Sabrina missed the rest of the game. I haven't heard how their mission went, but they'll be happy to know we won."

"Congratulations, Professor," said Addie.

"You'll be a much better player after your experience on Aquare, Star Girl," said Professor Nebulas. "All that floating is a lot like being in the spaceball courts, isn't it?"

"Yes, it is. I think the mission has helped me a lot," Addie agreed.

"Well, off you go, girls. Mission points will be sent to your SpaceBerries as usual."

★ ★ ★ ★

Back in the dorm room, Miya and Addie were on their laptops.

"Addie, why did you think I wouldn't want to call the holographic teacher on a mission?" Miya asked.

"Valentina told me that it's bad and you lose points," answered Addie.

"Everything is about points and winning with Valentina," said Miya. "I feel a little sorry for her. It must be really hard always needing to be the best."

"Yeah," said Addie. "I just want to get good enough grades to stay here. I think I'll do better in Zero Gravity class after the simulation tanks and going to Aquare. I hope so, anyway. Hey, my friend back home has just come on SpaceChat. I'm going to write to her."

"Okay," said Miya. "I'm going to upload those photos I took on Aquare."

Addie typed in a response to Jess on her laptop.

STAR GIRL
Yep, I just went on a mission with Miya. It was so good to go with a friend this time. ☺

JESS
That's awesome! I wish I could see where you go.

STAR GIRL

Me too. Hey, I'll send you some photos of a galaxy that I took today.

JESS

Cool!

STAR GIRL

I better go. I need to study. My grades aren't very good.

JESS

You need a study buddy like me up there on that space station.

STAR GIRL

I do! Miss you, Jess. CYA

JESS

CYA

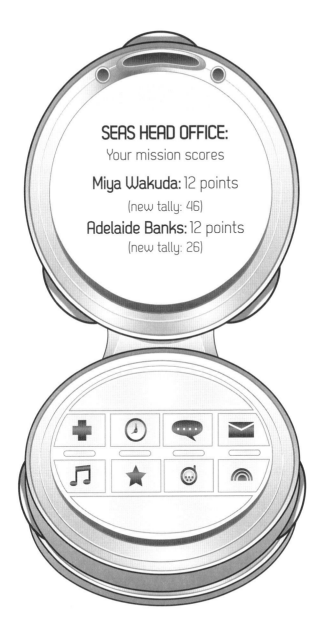

SEAS HEAD OFFICE:

Your mission scores

Miya Wakuda: 12 points

(new tally: 46)

Adelaide Banks: 12 points

(new tally: 26)

TOP TEN SPACE CADET SCOREBOARD

NAME	PHOTO	CADET POINTS	HOUSE
Valentina Adams (SC Supernova 1)		58	NEBULA
Grace Mauro (SC Comet XS)		50	NEBULA
Miyako Wakuda (SC Astron Girl)		46	NOVA
Louisa Jeffries (SC Star Cluster)		40	NOVA
Hannah Merrington (SC Galactic 6)		38	METEOR
Sabrina Simcic (SC Neuron Star)		38	NEBULA
Aziza Van De Walt (SC Asteroid)		35	NOVA
Lara Walsh (SC Red Giant)		28	METEOR
Adelaide Banks (SC Star Girl)		26	STELLAR
Olivia Marston (SC Orbital 2)		24	STELLAR

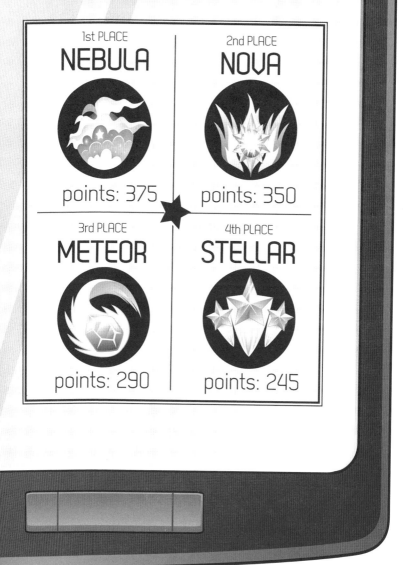

SCHOOL HOUSE SCOREBOARD

1st PLACE
NEBULA
points: 375

2nd PLACE
NOVA
points: 350

3rd PLACE
METEOR
points: 290

4th PLACE
STELLAR
points: 245

STAR ★ GIRL
SAVING SPACE ONE PLANET AT A TIME

Check out all of Star Girl's space adventures!